...d the Scenes
...th Coders

# MOBILE APPLICATIONS DESIGNER

### David Machajewski

**PowerKiDS** press.

New York

Published in 2018 by The Rosen Publishing Group, Inc.
29 East 21st Street, New York, NY 10010

First Edition

Editor: Melissa Raé Shofner
Book Design: Rachel Rising

Photo Credits: Cover, pp. 1, 3–32 (background) Lukas RS/Shutterstock.com; Cover, Scanrail1/Shutterstock.com; Cover, wavebreakmedia/Shutterstock.com; p. 5 ESB Professional/Shutterstock.com; p. 6 blinkblink/Shutterstock.com; p. 7 Africa Studio/Shutterstock.com; p. 9 Golubovy/Shutterstock.com; p. 11 George Dolgikh/Shutterstock.com; p.12 spaxiax/Shutterstock.com; p. 13 Ollyy/Shutterstock.com; p. 15 Karakagotgot/Shutterstock.com; p. 17 baranq/Shutterstock.com;p. 18 Run the Jewels/Shutterstock.com; p. 19 ronstik/Shutterstock.com; p. 21 Rawpixel.com/Shutterstock.com; p. 23 Jack Frog/Shutterstock.com; p. 25 REDPIXEL.PL/Shutterstock.com; p. 27 YAKOBCHUK VIACHESLAV/Shutterstock.com; p. 29 ProStockStudio/Shutterstock.com; p. 30 Julia Tim/Shutterstock.com.

Library of Congress Cataloging-in-Publication Data

Names: Machajewski, David.
Title: Mobile applications designer / David Machajewski.
Description: New York : PowerKids Press, 2018. | Series: Behind the scenes with coders | Includes index.
Identifiers: ISBN 9781508155768 (pbk.) | ISBN 9781508155706 (library bound) | ISBN 9781508155584 (6 pack)
Subjects: LCSH: Application software–Development–Juvenile literature. | Application software–Development. | Mobile computing–Juvenile literature.
Classification: LCC QA76.76.A65 M33 2018 | DDC 005.3–dc23

Manufactured in the United States of America

CPSIA Compliance Information: Batch #BS17PK: For Further Information contact Rosen Publishing, New York, New York at 1-800-237-9932

# Contents

# The Computer in Your Pocket

In 1969, NASA sent the first humans to the moon on the Apollo 11 mission. Large computers were used to guide the Saturn V rocket and help the astronauts on board communicate with the crew on Earth. These computers were very advanced for their time, and they cost millions of dollars to build.

It might be hard to believe, but a single smartphone—something that many of us carry in our pocket every day—is a computer that's much faster and more powerful than all of the computers owned by NASA in 1969 combined! Our phones and tablets are capable of doing amazing things. Today we can access millions of amazing tools on these devices with the tap of a finger. People called mobile **applications** designers build these tools.

Today's computers—including smartphones—are capable of doing things that would be considered impossible 50 years ago.

# Behind the Screen

Like any computer, the smartphones and tablets we use today contain software. Software is made up of code, which is a set of instructions that tells a computer to perform certain tasks. Computers are capable of many different tasks—from adding numbers to steering cars—if they have the right kind of software.

Men and women who write software go by many different titles, including "programmer," "coder," "developer," or "software engineer." The people who write code specifically for phones and tablets are called mobile applications designers. They write pieces of software called applications, or apps. If you've ever used a phone or tablet to play a game, get directions on a map, or watch a movie, then you've used a mobile app.

# Becoming an App Designer

How does someone become a mobile app designer? Many app designers have a college degree in computer science. Some companies that hire mobile app designers require such a degree. However, there are also ways to learn programming skills outside the classroom. You might teach yourself by studying online, or you might take part in a specialized training program.

The most important part of an app designer's education is learning to think like a programmer. Programming is all about critical thinking and problem solving. The first step to a career in mobile app design is building a strong foundation in these skills. Most computer-related education programs will require you to study and master different types of math and **logic**. Above all, the best way to become a good programmer is through lots of practice writing software.

Programmers usually start their education learning about computer science. Understanding how computers work is the first step to writing software.

9

# The Brain of the Phone

Beyond learning the basics of programming, mobile app designers also need to learn about the operating systems (OS) of the devices they work on. An operating system is the collection of advanced software that serves as the "brain" of a smartphone, tablet, or other computer. It sets the rules for how a user interacts with the device. It also manages all the device's resources so apps can run properly.

Mobile app designers need to be familiar with the operating systems of the devices they build apps for. The operating system used on Apple's mobile devices is iOS. Windows 10 Mobile is the OS built into Microsoft mobile devices. Android is a widely used OS developed by Google. It's used on phones and tablets manufactured by many leading **technology** companies.

## Tech Talk

Android and iOS are the two most popular mobile operating systems in use today. They're found on over 90 percent of all mobile devices in the United States. Most mobile app designers concentrate on these two systems.

All smartphones have an operating system. Mobile app designers need to be familiar with one or more of these platforms to code their apps.

# Open Source

The Android OS is special because it's an example of open-source software. "Open source" means that anybody in the world can access the Android OS software, experiment with it, modify it, and make improvements to the code. This makes it a very **flexible** operating system. It gives designers more freedom when building Android apps, which provides more options and variety for users.

# Tools of the Trade

Perhaps the most important skill a mobile app designer needs is knowledge of programming languages. While the operating system sets rules that a designer has to follow, a programming language is what they actually use to write an app.

A programming language is a set of rules and commands that app designers use to tell our phones or tablets what to do. Designers write statements in languages the computers in our devices can understand, just as you're able to understand the English language. To build an app, a designer writes a big "to-do" list for your phone or tablet in one of these languages. There are thousands of programming languages, but two of the most popular for writing mobile apps are Swift and Java.

Developers use programming languages to write directions that computers use to complete a set of actions.

## Lost in Translation

Programming languages are designed to communicate with computers. However, a computer doesn't understand these languages directly. Before a piece of software runs, the computer must translate the language into **binary code**. Binary code consists of long strings of 1s and 0s. These 1s and 0s tell the computer's **hardware** how to execute the developer's instructions.

# Look and Feel

Mobile developers need to be more than just good programmers. They need to build software that works well and looks good on the small touchscreens that control our phones and tablets. It's important that mobile app designers have a good understanding of **user experience (UX) design**.

UX is a term used by mobile app designers to describe how people interact with an app. Designers aim to build tools that are useful, fun to interact with, and easy to navigate. They're constantly thinking about how to make their apps fit cleanly on phone and tablet screens and function in ways that are self-explanatory. The best apps are often the simplest to use. Beyond having **technical** skills, mobile app designers need to be creative and care about the look and feel of an app.

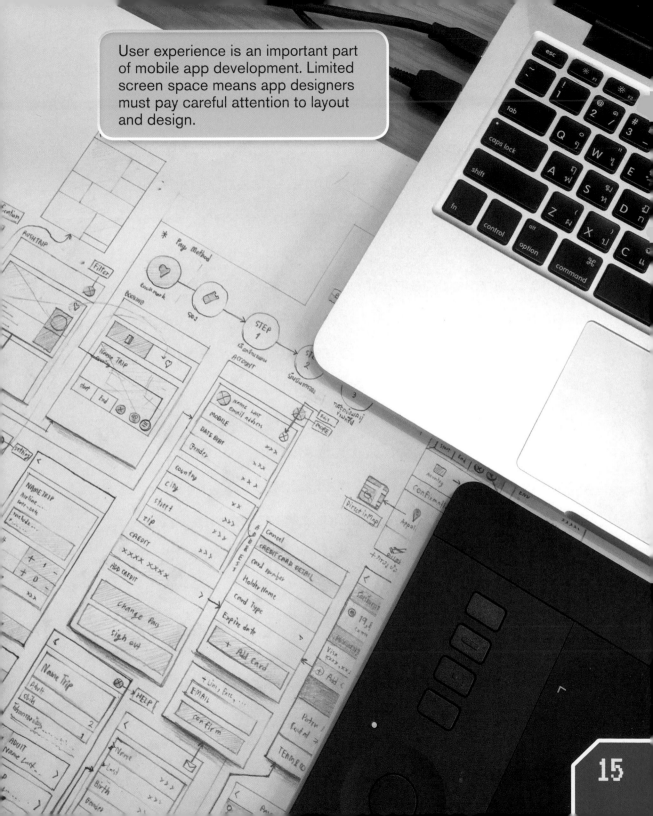

User experience is an important part of mobile app development. Limited screen space means app designers must pay careful attention to layout and design.

# Jack of All Trades

Mobile app designers do more than sit at a desk and write code all day. Companies that hire mobile developers search for candidates who have experience with several programming languages and software-writing methods. In addition, these languages and tools change all the time. This means mobile app developers need to be curious, eager to learn, and willing to solve new problems.

In the workplace, mobile app designers are also expected to be flexible and have strong communication skills. They may need to work on multiple projects at a time, and they often work with other team members. The best app designers are well rounded. Creativity and open-mindedness are very important when taking an idea and turning it into a working app.

Mobile app designers take an idea and turn it into a working piece of software. They need to be both technical and creative to build successful apps.

## Self-Starters

Mobile app designers showcase their skills by sharing examples of apps they've built in the past. Many work on personal projects in their spare time. This lets them practice their skills and learn new methods. Building your own apps is also a good way to show off your abilities to employers. Designers who work on their own projects stand out as skilled self-starters.

# In-Demand Skills

With more and more people using smartphones and tablets, there has been an increase in the use of mobile apps. This has created a huge demand for mobile app designers in the job market. Many companies see the need to provide mobile apps to their customers. At least 70 percent of organizations currently have some type of mobile product. All these companies need app designers to design and build their mobile products.

The need for mobile app designers has exploded over the past five years, and it continues to grow There are currently more job openings available in the market than there are qualified people to fill them. Salaries for this in-demand position are expected to increase over time.

Mobile technology has become very popular. There's a big need in the workplace for men and women who have the skills to write mobile apps.

19

# On the Job

What a mobile app designer does each day partly depends on the type of organization they work for. Companies offering mobile apps to their customers often hire mobile designers to work on staff. For instance, if a bank wants to provide its customers with a mobile banking application, the company might hire a team of mobile app designers as full-time employees to build and manage it.

Some organizations hire outside companies called development shops to handle their mobile app projects. A development shop has its own team of mobile app designers who work on projects for many different customers. Finally, many mobile app designers are self-employed. They build their own apps and sell them directly to users. They may also work on **freelance** projects in which they help others develop an app idea.

It's common for app designers to work as part of a team. Each designer works on a small part of a larger project.

# Billion-Dollar Ideas

Regardless of where they work, designers usually go through the same general process when building a mobile app. To start, a team will brainstorm ideas, decide what problem the app will solve, and figure out what resources are needed. App designers are involved in all stages of the process, but they're especially important when deciding if an idea is actually possible.

Every great app starts as an idea. Uber, a company worth over $28 billion, is based entirely around a mobile app. In 2008, Uber's founders realized it was sometimes difficult to hail a taxi. Their simple idea—an app with which people can request and pay for rides when needed—has changed the way we think about transportation in cities.

Coming up with a good idea is possibly the hardest part of designing an app. Original ideas can lead to big business in the world of mobile applications.

# Designing and Planning

Once a team settles on an idea for an app, the next step is to start designing. Mobile app designers usually begin this process by creating a wireframe. A wireframe is like a blueprint, or detailed plan. It's an illustration that shows how an app's features will look and function. Sometimes a team will build an app prototype, which is a wireframe you can interact with. At this stage, designers will also start thinking about how they want the finished app to look and feel.

App designers often share their prototype with users to get **feedback**. This lets designers know if the features and functions of an app make sense to other people. It also allows them to identify and fix any problems with their design before building the actual app.

Careful planning goes a long way in mobile app development. In the planning stage, designers think through all the problems and possibilities of an app so they're prepared when it comes time to start coding.

# Building and Testing

Once a team developer has decided on an app's design, it's time to build it. This phase is when app developers actually write the code. If they're working on a team, they'll typically split up the work. Each designer will focus on a specific part of the software.

After the first **version** of the software is completed, a team usually tests the app with users. Sometimes called beta testing, this is a critical process in which users are invited to try out a live version of the app and provide feedback to make sure it works like it's supposed to.

A big part of the building and testing process is debugging. Debugging is the process of identifying software errors, which programmers call "bugs," and fixing the code to correct the issues.

Writing the code for an app is a step-by-step process. During the building phase, app developers are constantly testing and debugging until everything works properly.

## Tech Talk

Anytime software is built, there will almost always be bugs that need to be fixed. Testing and debugging help designers correct problems before an app is made available to the public.

# Time for Launch

After an app is built and tested and designers are sure it's working properly, it's ready to be shared with the world. Nearly all apps are obtained through an app marketplace. Users browse, or look through, these marketplaces on their phone or tablet and **download** apps directly onto their device. Some app designers charge money to download their app, while other apps are available for free.

App marketplaces, such as Apple's App Store or Android's Google Play, are specific to the operating system on the user's device. They provide valuable information on all the apps, including user ratings and reviews. From games to business tools to social media, marketplaces contain mobile apps for just about anything you could imagine. If an app becomes popular in a marketplace, it can reach millions of people around the world.

App marketplaces let users explore millions of apps right in the palm of their hand.

# Tech Talk

● ● ●

Between the Apple and Android marketplaces, there are over 4 million apps available to smartphone and tablet owners. Gaming is currently the most popular category for Apple, making up almost one-fourth of the entire marketplace. As of mid-2016, there have been 65 billion total downloads reported from the Google Play Android marketplace and 140 billion reported from Apple's App Store.

# Mobile World, Mobile Future

With over half the world's population accessing the Internet from a mobile device and 56 percent of Internet traffic to major sites coming from mobile devices, there's no question we're living in a mobile world. As our computing habits shift from desktop computers to smartphones and tablets, mobile apps are powering the way we work and play every day.

As these trends continue to shape our society, there is perhaps no skill set more exciting than the ability to write mobile software. Men and women who build mobile apps create tools that help others with every aspect of their life. With a job market that continues to grow and a career that involves changing the world, the future for mobile app designers looks very bright.

# Glossary

**application (app):** A program that performs one of the major tasks for which a computer is used.

**binary code:** A type of information, made up entirely of the digits 1 and 0, that is directly understood by computers when running software.

**download:** Copy data from one computer to another, often over the Internet.

**hardware:** The physical parts of a computer system, such as wires, hard drives, keyboards, and monitors.

**feedback:** Information about reactions to something used as a basis for improvement.

**flexible:** Being able to move and bend in many ways; willing and able to change.

**freelance:** Done by a person who is independent and not a full employee of a company.

**logic:** A proper or reasonable way of thinking about or understanding something.

**technical:** Of or relating to a mechanical or scientific subject.

**technology:** A method that uses science to solve problems and the tools used to solve those problems.

**user experience (UX) design:** The work that makes using software or a web page as easy and pleasant as it can be.

**version:** A form of something that is different from the ones that came before it.

# Index

# Websites

Due to the changing nature of Internet links, PowerKids Press has developed an online list of websites related to the subject of this book. This site is updated regularly. Please use this link to access the list: www.powerkidslinks.com/bsc/mad